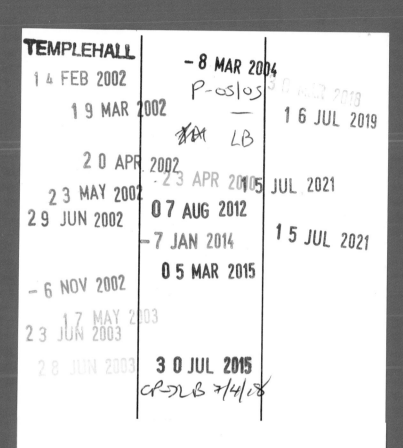

OXFORD
UNIVERSITY PRESS

Great Clarendon Street, Oxford OX2 6DP

Oxford University Press is a department of the University of Oxford.
It furthers the University's objective of excellence in research, scholarship,
and education by publishing worldwide in

Oxford New York

Athens Auckland Bangkok Bogotá Buenos Aires
Cape Town Chennai Dar es Salaam Delhi Florence Hong Kong Istanbul
Karachi Kolkata Kuala Lumpur Madrid Melbourne Mexico City Mumbai
Nairobi Paris São Paulo Shanghai Singapore Taipei Tokyo Toronto Warsaw

with associated companies in Berlin Ibadan

Oxford is a registered trade mark of Oxford University Press
in the UK and in certain other countries

First published 1998
First published in this edition 2001

British Library Cataloguing in Publication Data available

ISBN 0 19 272500 9

3 5 7 9 10 8 6 4 2

Printed in Malaysia

TREASURE ISLAND

Adapted and Illustrated by
Chris Mould

OXFORD
UNIVERSITY PRESS

The Old Buccaneer

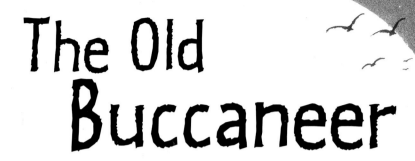

I shall not forget the day this adventure began. It was the day an old buccaneer swaggered to the door of our inn, dragging an old sea chest, singing as he went.

'Fifteen men on the dead man's chest,
Yo-ho-ho and a bottle of rum.'

My mother found a room for him, and there he stayed.

When he had nearly drowned himself in rum, he used to frighten the other drinkers with tales of storms at sea, and walking the plank.

'Jim,' he said to me one day, 'if ever you see a one-legged sailor, let me know at once.' And each day he sat waiting, and watching the ships in the harbour.

However, it was not the one-legged sailor who visited him, but a blind man named Pew. He tapped on the door with his stick, and asked for the old buccaneer.

I saw fear in the buccaneer's eyes as Pew grabbed him, pressed a paper into his palm, and left. He opened his hand and cried, 'It's the black spot! It's my old mates, Jim! They want my map!' And with that he collapsed and died, right there at my feet.

Now the buccaneer owed us a lot of money, so we opened his sea chest and took what was owed to us. I also found an oilskin packet which I took and hid inside my shirt.

That night we watched from outside, as Pew and his gang searched the inn for the papers I had in my shirt.

I took my mother to a safe place and then went to find our friend Dr Livesey at Squire Trelawney's house. I told them the story and we opened the packet. Inside was a map of an island with the signature: *J.F.*

'The infamous Captain Flint!' cried the squire. 'This map must show where his treasure is buried. Doctor, we are going to sea. Jim, you'll be cabin boy!'

He left for Bristol and soon wrote to tell us he had bought a ship. He had also hired a sea cook – a one legged man named Long John Silver, who was helping to find a crew.

The Sea Cook

I said goodbye to my mother and took the stagecoach to the port of Bristol. I met Long John Silver at the inn he owned.

We made our way through the winding streets down to the harbour and soon found our ship.

Boarding the *Hispaniola*, I was introduced to Mr Arrow, the first mate, and the ship's captain, Mr Smollett.

'There's talk on this ship,' said the captain to the squire and the doctor. 'I don't know how they found out, but there's talk of treasure and a map. You must be careful.'

'Pleased to meet you, Jim,' he said, shaking my hand. I liked him instantly.

I decided at that moment that I was none too keen on Captain Smollett. The anchor was lifted and the ship set sail.

The Voyage

I was filled with a feeling of adventure. But problems soon started. Mr Arrow began to stagger around the deck, mumbling incoherently, his eyes red.

I spent hours in the galley talking to Mr Silver, with his parrot, Captain Flint, on his shoulder.

Then one night he disappeared, presumably having fallen overboard.

'*Pieces of eight! Pieces of eight!*' it squawked.

One evening, feeling hungry, I went to the apple barrel. There was only one left so I climbed inside to reach it. It was quiet, and as the boat rocked gently on the waves I fell asleep curled up in the bottom.

I awoke to hear the voice of Silver. He was talking to young Dick and Israel Hands, and they were plotting to turn on the squire and his friends.

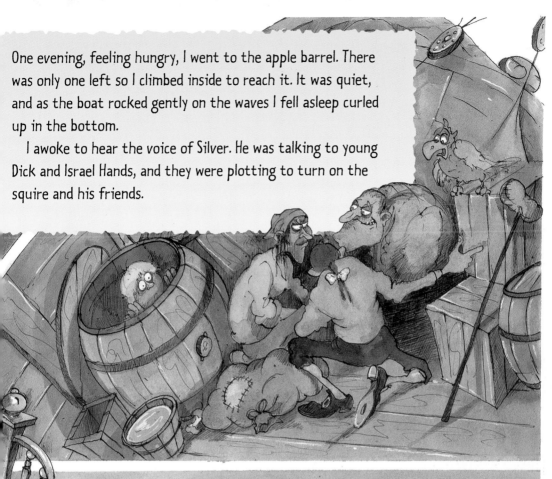

'It's best to wait until the treasure is on the ship and then do away with them,' Silver said.

A voice called from the crow's nest, 'Land ahoy!'

I told the captain, the squire, and the doctor of what I had heard.

'Well done, Jim,' said the captain. 'We'd best be careful from now on.'

The following morning I stood on the deck and looked at the place we called Treasure Island. We dropped anchor in the harbour and Captain Smollett allowed some of the men ashore. Silver was among them.

I also went ashore. Silver called to me but I ran off alone, across the beach and up into the woods.

After some time I heard the voice of Silver, bullying one of the sailors into joining the mutineers.

The man refused, but as he turned away, Silver took his crutch and hurled it into his back.

As he lay there gasping, Silver buried a knife through his coat. That was the end of him. Fearing for my life I ran frantically. He whom I had thought a kind and trusty man was the deadliest of pirates.

I ran into the trees and became lost. Eventually, I came upon a clearing, with a view of the harbour. Suddenly, something moved behind me.

Ben had been on Captain Flint's pirate ship. Three years earlier he had come back with some seamen to look for Flint's treasure. When they could not find it, the others grew angry and left Gunn on the island.

I told him Flint was dead, but when I told him that Silver was among our crew he gasped in horror.

Was it human? It darted from tree to tree, moving closer.
'Who are you?' I asked.

'Ben Gunn, marooned on this island for three years.'
And he told me his story.

We struck a bargain. If he helped us, we would take
him home. Just then we heard gunshots. We
spotted the Union Jack flying above a log house,
and I could see that my friends had left the
Hispaniola and were, for now, safe.

Mutiny

Our ship rocked in the harbour, with the Jolly Roger flying at her mast.

A group of pirates sat on the sand drinking rum.
I left Ben Gunn and climbed the fence around the log house to join my friends.

They were all there, and told me their story.
Smollett knew about the log house from Flint's
map, so with the faithful members of the crew
they took a boat and some supplies. The
mutineers saw them escape, and fired on the boat
until it sank. The men waded ashore, losing half of
their food and gunpowder.

The doctor explained that
the pirates' camp lay
near a swamp. This, and
the rum, would surely
make them ill. I told them
of my meeting with Ben
Gunn, and we agreed we
might need his help.

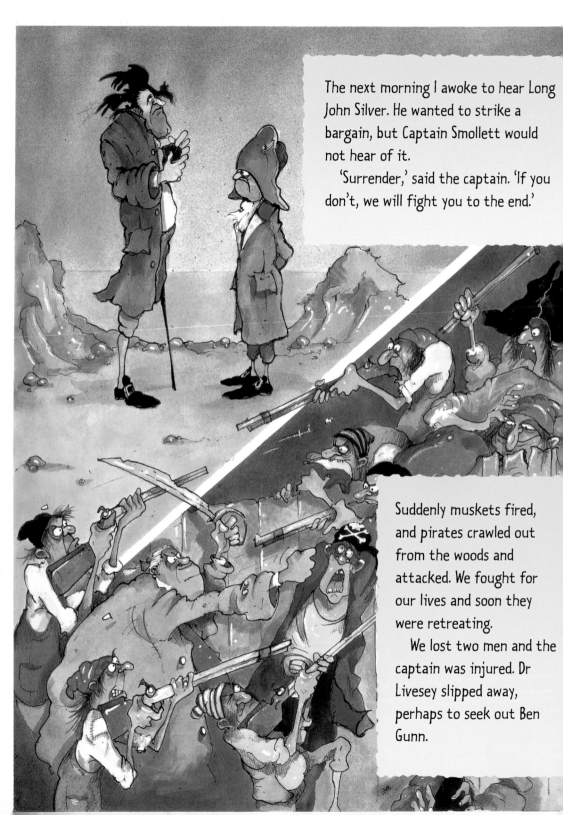

The next morning I awoke to hear Long John Silver. He wanted to strike a bargain, but Captain Smollett would not hear of it.

'Surrender,' said the captain. 'If you don't, we will fight you to the end.'

Suddenly muskets fired, and pirates crawled out from the woods and attacked. We fought for our lives and soon they were retreating.

We lost two men and the captain was injured. Dr Livesey slipped away, perhaps to seek out Ben Gunn.

I also left, taking two pistols, and ran down to the shore. Maybe if the pirates didn't find the treasure they would sail away, leaving us stranded. Ben Gunn had a small boat. If I could use it to get to the *Hispaniola*, I could cut the anchor and let the ship drift round to the other side of the island.

I reached the *Hispaniola* and eventually managed to grab the anchor rope. I cut through it with my knife and the ship was free.

The pirates on shore sang:
  '*Fifteen men on the dead man's chest,
  Yo-ho-ho and a bottle of rum.*'
I could also hear two pirates on the ship, arguing violently. One voice I knew well. It was Israel Hands.

In search of
Treasure

I bandaged my wound and waded ashore. I clambered up the hill to the log house. I opened the door and heard, '*Pieces of eight! Pieces of eight!*' It was Silver's parrot.

I tried to run, but Silver and his men held me. Where were my friends?

The pirates told me that Dr Livesey's men had given up the search for the treasure, and had given the map to them.

It was clear the men were growing tired of Silver. If they picked a new leader they would kill both him and me. He and I agreed that he would protect me, if I would approach Captain Smollett on his behalf.

The following morning Dr Livesey arrived to see the wounded pirates. I told him about my adventures with the ship and the bargain I had made with Silver.

After the doctor left, the pirates gathered their tools together and set off across the island in search of the treasure. But Silver was suspicious. Why had the map been handed over to them? Was it a trick?

The men were loaded with weapons and tools. I was tied at the waist to Silver.

Suddenly a shout came. At the foot of a tree was a skeleton.

'This is Flint's trickery,' said Silver. 'The bones point to the treasure.'

The thought of Flint made the men tremble.

'I wouldn't like to hear Flint's song now,' one whispered. Then we heard a high voice from the trees.

'Fifteen men on the dead man's chest,
Yo-ho-ho and a bottle of rum.'

'Flint's ghost!' cried one.

'Turn back!' said another.

But just then we came to the spot—an empty pit.

The treasure was gone.

Before the mutineers could turn on Silver, several of the pirates were felled by musket shots. As the surviving three ran off, Dr Livesey and Ben Gunn came out of the trees. They had saved us.

Pieces of Eight

We were taken to Ben Gunn's cave where we learned that the map had been of no use. Ben Gunn had found the gold years ago and moved it to his cave. When he had discovered this, the doctor was happy to hand the map over to the pirates.

The next morning there was much work to do, loading our riches onto the ship. We left supplies for the pirates who were still on the island, and sailed for home.

We stopped in South America to take on extra crew, and Silver disappeared, taking some of the money. Deep down we were glad.

We sailed home and shared our fortune. We never heard of Silver again.

But sometimes I dream I hear his parrot:

'Pieces of eight! . . .

'Pieces of eight! . . .'

andrew

Tips for Talking and Reading Together

Read at Home *Floppy's Phonics* stories are a fun and motivating way of using letter sounds to practise reading.

- Talk about the title and the picture on the cover.
- Identify the letter pattern *oo* and talk about the sound (phoneme) it makes when you read it.
- Look at the *oo* words on page 4. Say each word and then say the sounds in each word (e.g. *m-oo-n*).
- Read the story and find the words with *oo*.
- Discuss the Talk About ideas on page 21.
- Do the fun activity at the end of the book.

Have fun!

The
Moon Jet

Written by Roderick Hunt

Illustrated by Nick Schon,
based on the original characters
created by Alex Brychta

OXFORD

UNIVERSITY PRESS

Read these words

moon soon

cool shoot

zoom shoo

boom food

Kipper had a box and a bin.

Kipper got in his jet . . .

. . . and put on the lid.

"This jet is cool," said Kipper.

"Off I go," he said.

boom

boom

The jet shot off.

It shot out of the room.

"I will loop the loop,"
said Kipper.

The jet did six loops.

"I will go to the moon,"
said Kipper.

"I can get to it soon,"
he said.

The jet got to the moon.

But the moon bugs ran up.

"Yuk," said Kipper.

"Moon bugs."

"Shoo, get off," said Kipper.

"Did I nod off?" said Kipper.
"Yes," said Mum. "Get up to
bed."

Talk about the story

Where did Kipper go in his jet?

What happened when he got there?

How did Kipper make his jet?

Where would you go if you had a jet?

A maze

Help Kipper to get to the moon.

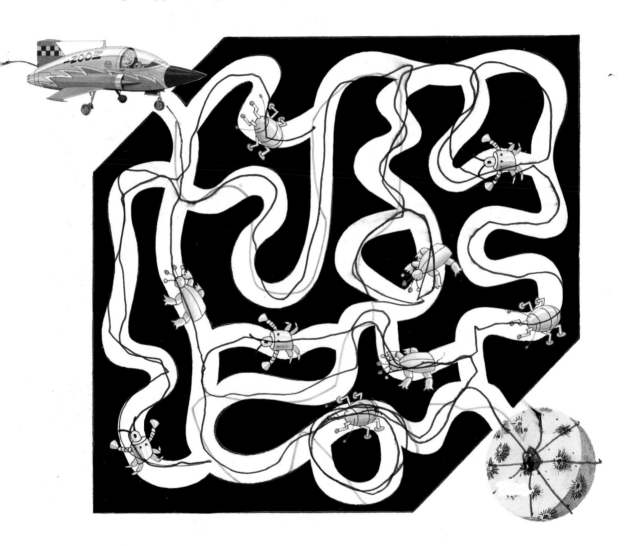

More books for you to enjoy

Have more fun with Read at Home

OXFORD
UNIVERSITY PRESS

Great Clarendon Street,
Oxford OX2 6DP

Text © Roderick Hunt 2009
Illustrations © Nick Schon and
Alex Brychta 2009

First published 2009
All rights reserved

British Library Cataloguing
in Publication Data available

ISBN: 9780198387398

10 9 8 7 6 5 4 3 2 1

Printed in China by Imago